KIDS CAN'T STOP READING
THE CHOOSE YOUR
OWN ADVENTURE® STORIES!

"Choose Your Own Adventure is the best thing that has come along since books themselves."
—Alysha Beyer, age 11

"I didn't read much before, but now I read my Choose Your Own Adventure books almost every night."
—Chris Brogan, age 13

"I love the control I have over what happens next."
—Kosta Efstathiou, age 17

"Choose Your Own Adventure books are so much fun to read and collect—I want them all!"
—Brendan Davin, age 11

And teachers like this series, too:
"We have read and reread, worn thin, loved, loaned, bought for others, and donated to school libraries our Choose Your Own Adventure books."

CHOOSE YOUR OWN ADVENTURE®—
AND MAKE READING MORE FUN!

Bantam Books in the Choose Your Own Adventure® Series
Ask your bookseller for the books you have missed.

TERROR IN AUSTRALIA

BY SHANNON GILLIGAN

ILLUSTRATED BY HOWARD SIMPSON

BANTAM BOOKS
TORONTO • NEW YORK • LONDON • SYDNEY • AUCKLAND

RL 5, IL age 10 and up
TERROR IN AUSTRALIA
A Bantam Book / July 1988

*CHOOSE YOUR OWN ADVENTURE® is a registered trademark of
Bantam Books, a division of Bantam Doubleday Dell Publishing
Group, Inc. Registered in U.S. Patent and Trademark
Office and elsewhere.*

Original conception of Edward Packard

*Interior art by Howard Simpson
Cover art by David Mattingly*

ISBN 0-553-27277-2

Published simultaneously in the United States and Canada

*Bantam Books are published by Bantam Books, a division of Bantam
Doubleday Dell Publishing Group, Inc. Its trademark, consisting of the
words "Bantam Books" and the portrayal of a rooster, is Registered in
U.S. Patent and Trademark Office and in other countries. Marca Regis-
trada. Bantam Books, 666 Fifth Avenue, New York, New York 10103.*

PRINTED IN THE UNITED STATES OF AMERICA

O   0 9 8 7 6 5 4 3 2 1

TERROR IN AUSTRALIA

WARNING!!!

Do not read this book straight through from beginning to end! These pages contain many different adventures you may have when you join your uncle, a famous archaeologist, in his search for an ancient civilization.

From time to time as you read along you will be able to make choices. Your choice may lead to success or disaster.

The adventures you have will be the results of those choices. After you make your choice, follow the instructions to see what happens to you next.

Beware! Your expedition to the Outback could prove deadly!

You open your eyes and stretch lazily, expecting to hear the muffled sounds of your parents making breakfast downstairs. Then you remember: your mom and dad left Australia yesterday for a three-week vacation in the United States. For the first time in your life, you're on your own!

"Just think, Ned," you say to your cat while you get ready to brush your teeth. "Three whole weeks to live it up." A few minutes later, you've put the kettle on for tea and are about to pour yourself a glass of orange juice when you hear a knock at the front door.

Ned stops licking his paws long enough to follow you as you answer it.

"Hi, Waldo," you say cheerily. Waldo, your neighbor and friend, delivers the newspaper every morning. "What's up?"

"Aren't you related to Gilroy Adams, the archaeologist?" he asks.

"He's my mother's youngest brother," you reply. "Why?"

"Here," Waldo says, handing you the paper. "He's made the front page of today's *Melbourne Age*. And probably a lot of other papers. Thought you'd be interested."

"Thanks," you say curiously as Waldo heads off to finish his route.

Turn to page 2.

You unroll the newspaper. The picture on the first page is Gilroy, all right. You read the article:

"Gilroy Adams, twenty-year-old renegade archaeologist, holds an amulet that he claims is proof of Satyrion, a highly developed ancient civilization, the capital of which is believed to have been located in the middle of the Gibson Desert. Adams reports that the amulet was discovered by an aboriginal friend on walkabout in the region. Initial analysis of the piece indicates that it is made of a substance heretofore unknown to man.

"Mr. Adams is the youngest archaeologist ever to graduate . . ."

Before you finish the article, the phone rings.

"Gilroy!" you exclaim, when you hear your uncle's voice on the line. "I was just reading about the amulet in the paper. You made the front page of *Melbourne Age*. That's really exciting!"

"Thanks, kiddo," your uncle replies. "Exciting is the word, all right. Maybe *too* exciting. I think I need your help."

Turn to page 6.

"Oof! This pack is *heavy*," groans Waldo as he helps you carry your things to the cab.

"Where'll it be?" asks the driver, opening the trunk of her cab.

"The train station, please," you reply. Turning to your friend, you add, "You never know when extra cash will come in handy."

"Be careful," Waldo says, giving you a shy hug. "Watch out for wild camels. And *please* don't be late coming home."

"Oh, I won't," you say breezily. "I hope," you add to yourself.

A half hour later, you're comfortably settled in a second class sleeping car. The Melbourne Star lurches slowly from the train station. You look at your watch. Right on schedule, you think. Your search for the lost city of Satyrion has begun.

Turn to page 8.

"Gilroy! You're alive!" you yell. You leap from the helicopter without looking—and land on your face in the sand. You pick yourself up and race toward your uncle. "What *happened* to you?" you say excitedly.

But something is terribly wrong. Your uncle stares at you vacantly. His expression is so blank that for a minute you wonder if you've made a mistake. "Gilroy?" he repeats. "Who's Gilroy?"

Bininuwuy is in the same state. He doesn't even recognize Mandarg.

"Fortren!" exclaims the medic who came along in your helicopter. He's standing next to a water drum, a suspicious look on his face. "Their water must have been drugged."

"What's Fortren?" you ask Major Symington.

"It's a drug that kills memory. All memory. It can last for several days. The Brotherhood of Allah uses it frequently. I'm afraid there's no chance of being led to that hideout now," he says, kicking the sand. "By the time your uncle and his friend recover their memories, those terrorists will be long gone."

The End

6

"My help?" you reply. "What's wrong?" You and Gilroy have always been close, and he has seemed much more like a cousin or friend than an uncle. You know that Gilroy trusts you completely.

"Nothing's wrong . . . yet," Gilroy replies. "Just suspicions. But I can't talk on the phone. We need to meet in person. Can you come to Alice Springs? My expedition leaves from here in two days."

Your heart jumps at your uncle's words. You've wanted to go on an expedition with Gilroy for as long as you can remember, but your parents have never allowed it. As your father is fond of saying, "Gilroy's got kangaroos in the top of his paddock."

But this time, your parents aren't here.

"Will I be back in three weeks?" you ask, crossing your fingers.

"Sure, we can arrange that," Gilroy replies.

"I'm on!" you cry.

Gilroy gives you the address of his hotel.

"I'll be there as soon as I can," you promise before hanging up.

Turn to page 10.

SCREECH!

You slam on your brakes, trying to avoid two vehicles that have been parked on the other side, blocking the narrow track. A helicopter is parked in the distance.

"Going somewhere?" asks Major Winks. He's dressed in fatigues—and he's pointing a pistol straight at your heart.

The End

You pull out a beginner's guide to archaeology and try to read, but you're just too excited. At last you decide to go to the dining car and have a bite to eat instead.

You move carefully through the narrow corridors, swaying gently with the train.

Whomp! A short, pasty-looking man veers around a corner and plows right into you.

"Excuse me, sir," you say politely, trying to help the man back to his feet.

He furiously clutches a worn black briefcase to his chest and squirms from your touch. "Leave me alone! I can get up myself!" he barks in a heavy accent that you can't identify. Then he shoves you out of the way and hurries off.

"What was the matter with *him*?" you wonder. "He acted as if I'd tried to steal his stupid briefcase!"

Turn to page 14.

10

Later that morning, you're busily packing for your trip while your neighbor Waldo and Ned, your cat, look on.

"What happens if your parents find out where you've gone?" Waldo asks nervously.

"If you take good care of Ned and the house and keep quiet about my trip, they'll never find out," you answer.

"What do I tell them if you're not home in three weeks?"

"It won't matter," you reply with a smile, "because if I'm not home in three weeks, my parents will kill me."

Waldo rolls his eyes. "How are you traveling to Alice Springs?" he wants to know.

"I haven't made up my mind. The train is cheaper, but if I go that way I won't get there till tomorrow morning. If I take a plane, I won't have any money left over, but I'll be in Alice by dinner."

Beep, beep!

The taxi you called is announcing its arrival.

"You've got to decide soon," Waldo points out.

"I'll decide right now," you tell him.

If you decide to go to Alice Springs by train, turn to page 3.

If you decide to go by plane, turn to page 18.

A short while later, the other members of your team amble back into camp. You overhear Jim Dodds talking to Major Winks.

"The kid's fooled for now," he says, "but what happens when we begin mining?"

"Don't worry. We'll figure out some creative method of disposal," the so-called major Winks replies. "Praise be to Allah that things have gone well so far."

Turn to page 62.

You check the hallway one last time. Then—slowly, silently—you bend down, trying not to wake the sleeping figure. You pick up the papers farthest from his feet and begin scanning them. They appear to be some sort of technical readouts, almost like a seismogram. In the upper left corner of each paper is stamped:

Classified and Restricted
U.S. Department of Defense

The U.S. Department of Defense? But this guy isn't American! What's he doing with classified information from the U.S. defense department?

At that moment the man groans in his sleep and shifts position. The heel of his shoe slams down onto your hand. It's all you can do not to yelp in pain. Moving very carefully, you lift his heel and pull your hand back.

For the second time that night you get the surprise of your life. On the paper that was underneath the man's heel is your uncle's name!

Turn to page 25

You reach the dining car and order a double coffee milkshake. As you drink you forget the strange man. You're lost in daydreams of the artifacts you'll find with Gilroy and the mysteries that lie ahead, waiting to be unraveled.

"Dining car's closing," a voice says.

"Wha—what?" you ask, coming back to reality.

"I said, the dining car's closing. It's eleven o'clock," a waiter tells you.

"Oh, yes. Sorry," you say, rubbing your eyes. Outside a dark, starry sky speeds past. You must have fallen asleep.

You stand up, leave a tip on your table, and head back to your seat. Passing through the first-class cars, you spot the odd little man that you bumped into. He's alone in his compartment and appears to be sound asleep. His precious briefcase has fallen out of his grasp and opened. Papers are fanned out all over the floor near his feet.

You feel a sudden urge to look at the papers. Just what's so important about them? You glance stealthily up and down the corridor. No one is in sight, and if someone does come along, you could easily pretend you're picking up the papers.

But what if the man wakes up and recognizes you? What if he's not asleep at all?

If you decide to look at the man's papers under the pretext of picking them up for him, turn to page 13.

If you decide to leave his papers where they are, turn to page 27.

The mail plane is a small, six-seat Piper Cub. It makes five stops between Melbourne and Alice Springs as the pilot and copilot drop off and pick up mail, supplies, and an occasional passenger.

"Today we're also stopping at a cattle station to deliver some emergency allergy medicine," the pilot tells you cheerfully.

You smile at him, but you're wondering if you have *any* chance of making it to Alice Springs by tonight.

It turns out you have nothing to worry about.

As soon as you're airborne, you decide to use the flying time to get some extra sleep. When you wake up, there's only one more stop to make. It's at a tiny airport—nothing more than a landing strip and control tower. The pilot and copilot, Ed and Gerry, get out to have some pie and coffee. They politely invite you to join them, but you decline. Instead you phone the hotel in Alice Springs and leave a message for Gilroy saying that you should be there within the hour.

"Ready to go?" Gerry asks, just as you're finishing the call.

"You bet," you reply, hanging up the receiver.

Turn to page 19

You toss and turn uncomfortably for the rest of the night. When the Melbourne Star pulls into the Alice Springs station in the morning, you feel anything but rested.

You lug your bags onto the platform and scan the crowd for your uncle. You don't see him anywhere, but in a minute a young woman dressed in loose khaki clothing approaches you.

"Your uncle Gilroy sent me," she informs you. "I'm Anna Williams." She smiles, extending her hand.

"My uncle sent you?" you ask. You recall the odd events of last night and suddenly are filled with suspicion.

"Yes. He asked me to take you back to the hotel and brief you along the way," she replies, reaching for one of your bags.

"Why should I trust you?" you challenge her. "My uncle didn't say anything about someone else meeting me."

"Please! It's for your own good," Anna says quietly.

Turn to page 28.

18

You give Ned a good-bye pat, then you and Waldo carry your bags to the waiting cab. One look at the cloudless January sky and you're glad you decided to fly.

"Anyway," you say to Waldo, "the sooner I'm in Alice, the better."

"Be careful," Waldo tells you for the tenth time.

"I will," you promise. "I really appreciate your help, Waldo! I couldn't do this without you."

Turn to page 49.

You haven't been in the air long when Ed says, "Where the heck did *that* come from?"

Something in his voice makes you look up from the book you've started reading. Straight ahead is a large, mean-looking storm cell.

"The weather report said all clear when we took off!" Gerry tells Ed.

"Call Alice. See what they say," Ed directs.

A few seconds later Gerry replies, "They say there's nothing on their weather maps."

"What is it, then?" Ed asks.

The small craft begins to bounce uneasily. A little nervously you check your seat belt to make sure it's fastened. You wish you weren't the only passenger now.

Suddenly the air grows very dark. Raindrops begin to drum the metal skin of the aircraft— lightly at first, then in force. Lightning crackles outside the window.

You look at the faces of the two pilots. Is it your imagination that they're turning green?

Turn to page 95.

Someone taps you on the shoulder. Startled, you turn around.

"Gilroy! Am I glad to see you!" you exclaim, hugging your uncle hello.

"Glad to see you, too," Gilroy replies. "Boy, am I glad you came by plane. You must be clairvoyant. Right after we talked this morning, I decided we had to leave today. If you had come by train, I would have had to wait until tomorrow, at the earliest. Let's get your luggage and I'll take you to meet the others."

"The others?" you repeat.

"Bininuwuy, my aboriginal tracker-friend who found the amulet. He's been my guide for my last three trips into the bush. And Ophelia Redburn. She's a colleague of mine on the archaeological trail," Gilroy replies.

Moments later, you are seated in Gilroy's Jeep, hurtling through the streets of Alice Springs.

Turn to page 96.

"Everyone calls me Fifi," Ophelia tells you, shaking your hand vigorously.

"Hey, there!" says Bininuwuy softly, giving you a wave and a shy smile.

You notice that the Jeeps are already packed with food, water, extra gas, camping supplies, and archaeological equipment. Everyone seems eager to get going, so Gilroy starts issuing last-minute directions. While he and Bininuwuy are talking, Fifi gives you a wink. It seems conspiratorial. Or are you imagining things? She *does* remind you of someone, but who?

Your thoughts are interrupted by your uncle, who says that it's time to leave. As the Jeep pulls onto the road, he asks how much you know about Satyrion.

"Not much," you admit.

"I'll start at the top, then," Gilroy responds. "You'll need some background information."

Turn to page 103.

Three hours later, the real Gilroy sits beside your hospital bed. Your left leg is broken. You'll be in traction for the next several days. And in a cast for weeks.

"This whole thing was probably getting too dangerous for you anyway," your uncle says.

"What do you mean? I still don't know what's going on! Tell me what's happening," you plead.

"I can't say anything yet. But eventually it will be in the newspapers. If I were you, I'd spend my time figuring out a way to explain all this to your parents," says Gilroy, chuckling.

The End

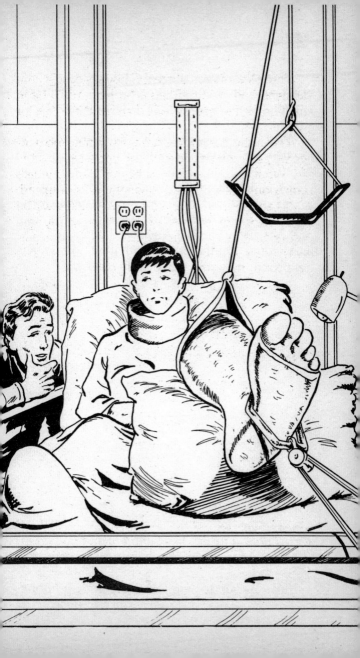

"A rescue? You think we'll be rescued? They don't even know where we went down. I never got to radio Alice. A rescue could take weeks!" you say.

"Well," Ed replies, "the first rule in a situation like this is to stay with your plane." Then he passes out.

You look around at the wrecked plane. Despite what Ed's just told you, you want desperately to find help. If you were alone, you'd do it in a second. Your only worry is leaving Ed, since he's sick and injured. On the other hand, if he doesn't get help soon, he could really be in trouble.

If you decide to risk leaving the plane and go in search of help, turn to page 40.

If you decide to stay with the plane and hope for a rescue, turn to page 101.

You begin reading furiously, but you're so nervous that you can hardly make out the words. Something about uranium. A mention of Satyrion. And a mention of Infiltrator IV—whatever that is.

It's impossible to tell what part your uncle plays in all this. Could the papers have anything to do with the trouble he's in?

You wonder if you'd be able to understand these documents better with more time to study them. The odd little man is still asleep—you dart a glance at him to check—and it would be easy to leave the compartment with his precious papers. But what would happen if he discovered that they were missing?

*If you decide to grab the papers,
turn to page 80.*

*If you decide to leave the papers for now and
follow the man when you get off in Alice
Springs, turn to page 69.*

You walk right by the papers. "If that weirdo were to wake up," you think, "he'll probably call the railway police or something."

You continue to your sleeping compartment. Once in bed, you are quickly rocked to sleep by the train. Several hours later, a clicking noise in the hallway jerks you awake. Someone is trying to pick the lock on your compartment door!

As you lie there, frozen, the train zooms by a station. For a split second you see the silhouette of a tall, heavyset figure against the light. Then it's gone. By the time you clamber out of your bunk and check the hallway, no one is there.

Should you tell a porter what just happened? You finally decide not to. The lock looks fine, and you're not sure anyone would believe your story. The porter might just think you'd been dreaming—and as you stare down the quiet hallway, you're not sure you haven't been.

"I'll be glad when we get to Alice Springs," you think with a shudder.

Turn to page 17.

You're going to feel pretty stupid if you get back to the hotel and this woman does indeed turn out to work for Gilroy. On the other hand, you're really spooked by the events on the train and that figure outside your door last night. Someone is out to get you. You can just feel it. For all you know, it could be this woman.

If you tell Anna Williams that you'd feel safer meeting her at the hotel, turn to page 65.

If you decide to take your chances and accept a ride with Anna, turn to page 34.

"Ooooh," someone groans in pain. After a moment, you realize it's you. You're tied to a chair in an unbearably hot, airless room. A large gash on your forehead has swollen your right eye shut. "Help me," you whimper softly.

In the next room, you hear a door opening and the footsteps of several people entering. "Is the kid awake yet?" someone asks. You think it's the woman from the cab, but you're not positive.

"Nah. Not the last time I looked. Any luck with the camels?" a man replies.

Before there's an answer, someone moves toward the door to the room you're in. You watch as the handle slowly starts to turn.

Turn to page 106.

"Yes. An aborigine who's skilled in the old ways can survive surprisingly well in almost all parts of the outback," Gilroy answers. "Anyway, one night Bininuwuy had a dream. In it he found an amulet buried a foot deep or so. It was near a peculiarly shaped cluster of cacti."

A chill runs down your spine. You remember the man from the plane and his strange message: "When you get into the desert near the cacti, continue another two-point-seven miles north-north-east."

"The next day, Bininuwuy found the cacti from the dream and started to dig nearby. Sure enough—" your uncle is saying, but you interrupt him.

"Gilroy, does anyone else know about this? I mean how Bininuwuy found the amulet?"

"No. No one besides you. And Bininuwuy, of course. I haven't even told Fifi yet."

"I have something important to tell you," you begin.

Turn to page 107.

Gilroy stares after the disappearing plane. "We've been tricked," he announces grimly.

"But by whom?" you ask.

"Who knows?" Gilroy replies. "My guess is that Major Winks and his friends are members of the Brotherhood of Allah themselves."

"And they're about to mine enough uranium to take control of the entire planet," you add, saying what all of you are thinking. "What can we do?"

"I don't know, but we certainly can't radio for help," Gilroy says, fiddling with the shortwave you just unloaded. "They've taken the precaution of removing the batteries."

"Hey, boss?" Bininuwuy says. "I've got a confession to make."

"Not now, Bininuwuy, not now," your uncle replies grumpily.

But that doesn't faze his friend. "The Brotherhood of Allah stole the batteries," he says with a huge grin, "but I stole them back." He pulls them out with a flourish.

Turn to page 113.

You've been hit by lightning!

The blast blows out the entire instrument panel. The dashboard before you is a worthless, smoking mess. Meanwhile, the storm rages, and the little plane is tossed around like a leaf in the wind.

You're fighting off panic. Just try to maintain altitude for now, you repeat over and over to yourself. You'll have to do it by feel. Every time the plane seems to ascend or descend, you try to make an adjustment. But this tactic won't work forever. The fuel tanks were low when you took off—and you'll have to land sometime.

Sure enough, the engines begin to sputter several minutes later. You have no choice. You *must* land. Frantically you search for an opening in the clouds. There's one! A patch, lighter gray than the rest, emerges ahead.

You go for it. Pushing the wheel forward, you put the plane in a shallow glide path to earth and watch the airspeed to prevent stall.

Suddenly you're below the clouds—and dropping. The last thing you remember is the earth rushing up to meet you.

You pass out before you hit the ground.

Turn to page 70.

"I may be sorry for this," you say with a sigh, "but I'll come."

"Good," Anna replies with a big smile. "I promise that you're doing the right thing."

She grabs your heaviest bag and heads for the parking lot. You notice that she keeps a discreet eye on the crowd, as if she's looking for someone. Or watching out. But nothing happens. Anna leads you cheerfully to a shiny new Land Rover, throws your things in the back, and expertly maneuvers into the traffic.

"Well?" you say after driving for several minutes in silence. "My briefing?"

"I don't really work for your uncle. Not directly, anyway," she begins.

"Great. Just great. I walked right into a trap!" you say bitterly.

"You don't understand." Anna tries to give you a reassuring smile. "I'm with Australian intelligence. I've been assigned to your uncle's case."

"My uncle's case?" you repeat. But Alice Springs is a small town, and before Anna can continue, you've pulled up to the Barker House Hotel.

"Come on. I'll tell you everything in the room," she replies.

Go on to the next page.

Without stopping at the front desk, Anna leads you up the central staircase to a room on the second floor. A familiar figure sits on the bed talking on the phone, his back to you.

"Gilroy!" you exclaim.

The figure turns—but it's not Gilroy at all. It's someone who looks just like him. Behind you, you hear the click of the door being shut. You break into a cold sweat. What's going on? The man hangs up the phone and comes toward you with a warm smile.

If you decide to make a run for it, turn to page 76.

If you decide to wait and see if there's an explanation for the morning's strange events, turn to page 51.

It's hunger, not Anna, that finally awakens you. You look around and realize that everyone is gone! The Jeeps are still there, some tents have been erected, a pot boils on the fire, but where is everyone?

"Anna? Major Winks?" you call. No one answers. You walk over to a little rise nearby to get a view of things.

When you first spot the others, your only feeling is relief, and you start to run toward them. But immediately you stop dead in your tracks: all seven are kneeling on prayer rugs pointed west, the direction of Mecca! In low voices they wail melancholy Islamic prayers.

Instinctively you run back to your bedroll and pretend to be asleep. What does this *mean*?

Turn to page 11.

The two leave the room to confer. When they return a few minutes later, two tough-looking young men come with them.

"We are going to a camel farm. We wish to purchase at least eleven camels. Since you know camels, you will negotiate," Hans announces tersely.

"Then what?" you demand.

"Then you will be let go to continue your holiday," the woman tells you.

Somehow you don't think Grandma here is telling the truth, but what say do you have in the matter?

The toughs untie your hands and feet and lead you outside. You are surprised to find that their "hideout" is just a regular house in a regular neighborhood. Some regular-looking kids are playing on bikes across the street.

Seeing them gives you an idea.

You are surrounded by the four adults, but your hands and feet are free. If you move fast and run for it, you could reach the kids. Maybe they would help you. There are so many of them that your captors couldn't kidnap them, too.

If you decide to try making an escape, turn to page 63.

If you decide to bide your time because there's bound to be another opportunity to escape later, turn to page 42.

You wait nervously for one hour, then two. There's no sign of your uncle. Where can he be? To pass the time, you pull out the news clipping from yesterday's paper and re-read the article.

". . . Adams reports that the amulet was discovered by an aboriginal friend . . ."

Mention of Gilroy's aboriginal friend gives you an idea.

"Excuse me," you say again to the receptionist. "Isn't there an aboriginal settlement in Alice?" You have no idea when Gilroy will show up. You might as well see if you can learn a little about the aborigines here.

"Yes," the woman replies. She gives you directions and shows you a map advertising the tourist attractions of Alice Springs. You leave a message for your uncle in case he shows up, and then take off. A half hour later, you are showing his picture to a group of aborigines.

Turn to page 45.

Your instincts tell you that going for help is the only thing to do. Fifteen minutes later you're ready. Strapped to your back is your pack. It contains one of the gallons of water, some freeze-dried food you had packed for the expedition, and your sleeping bag. In your hand is an old compass. The last thing you do is leave a note pinned to Ed stating your intended direction, the date, and the time. Taking your bearings, you face northeast and begin walking.

You walk all day, pausing twice to drink a little water. The sandstorm never lets up, and before long your exposed skin is raw. Even so, you're not discouraged. A powerful sense of direction guides your steps. You don't know what it is, but you feel almost elated by what's happening to you.

At dusk, you take shelter against a large rock. You feel faint and dizzy. "I'll be much better after a few hours of sleep," you think, climbing into your bag. Around you the sandstorm rages on.

By the time you wake up, the sun is high overhead. You must have been more tired than you thought. The storm has stopped, and the quiet is almost eerie. You stand up to stretch. It is then that you first notice it: a few feet away, the sand has exposed a vein of metal that gleams in the light. You step closer and kick some more sand aside. The vein gets bigger. Then it hits you: it's gold!

Turn to page 94.

Shortly thereafter, Hans gives you a special injection. You never regain consciousness. Your destiny, like your corpse, becomes a buried secret.

A thousand years in the future, a young archaeologist comes across your skeleton. "Ah," she says to herself, "more proof of that ancient civilization, Australia."

The End

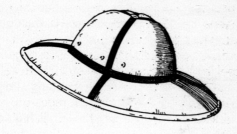

Carefully noting the house number and street name so you can report the location of the hideout later, you climb into the car.

Hans drives the sedan to the outskirts of town. He turns off at a ratty old sign that says: Wilhelm's Camels—for Rent by the Hour.

The toughs push you out of the car to do your job, and you go off in search of Wilhelm. But Wilhelm, it turns out, is away for the day. He won't be back till late that night.

"Can I take a look at the camels anyway?" you ask a ranch hand who's not much older than you.

"I guess so," he replies. He leads you to the paddock. Hans and the old woman make an attempt to follow you inside, but the ranch hand bolts the gate before they can enter. "Sorry. Only one at a time. Too many visitors make the camels nervous."

Turn to page 61.

The furniture van is actually filled with furniture, so you find a comfortable couch to lie on and settle in for a silent ride to Gilroy's hideout. It's growing dark by the time you arrive, but you can see enough to tell that you've been brought to some kind of cattle station. No other houses are in sight. Anna and Jim lead you inside. And there—at last—is your uncle.

"Gilroy!" you shout, running to him and giving him a huge hug.

"Sorry about this," your uncle says. "Intelligence got to me after I called you. There was no way to inform you safely over the phone."

"What's going on?" you ask for the hundredth time in the last two days.

"I'm probably the best person to answer that question," says an older man, standing up from his chair in the corner. "Tom Winks is my name—Major Tom Winks. I'm head of military intelligence for the Northern Territory and commander of this operation. Why don't you have a seat?"

Turn to page 58.

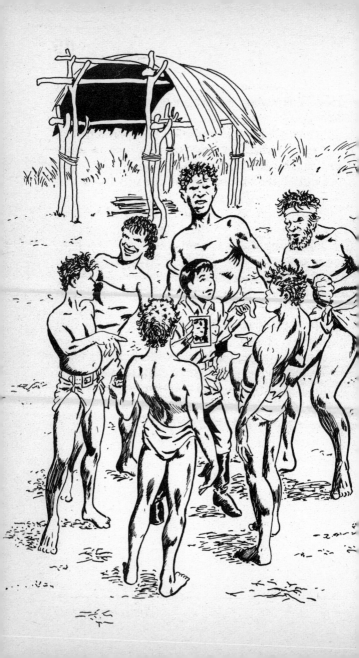

"Sure, we know your uncle. He's a good guy. He's Bininuwuy's friend," an eager young man tells you.

"Have you seen him? Recently?" you ask.

"Yes," replies a much older man. "This morning, just before he and Bininuwuy left."

Left! "Left for where!" you cry.

Turn to page 77.

"I'd like to help catch these awful people," you tell the assembled group.

"Good." The major nods and smiles. "We thought we could count on you."

The only thing you feel badly about is putting off your first expedition with Gilroy. But your uncle makes you feel better. "We'll be spending most of our time supporting your group anyway," he tells you. "I'm really proud of you," he adds, beaming.

In a short while the plane depositing Gilroy and his team in the desert takes off. You are given a comfortable cot to sleep on, and soon you're sound asleep.

Turn to page 52.

Some days later the doctors sadly inform you that your uncle's expedition has been discovered abandoned in the middle of the Gibson Desert. There was no sign of life anywhere.

The End

When you reach the Melbourne airport, you find out that the next flight to Alice Springs leaves in four hours.

"And it's booked solid," the ticket clerk tells you. "If you'd like to take it, you'll have to fly standby."

"Standby!" you cry. "But I have to get to Alice tonight!"

"Why don't you see if there's a space on the mail plane?" she suggests. "Go to the last desk before baggage pickup."

You hurry over to where she pointed. Sure enough, a mail flight destined for Alice Springs is about to leave.

"It makes lots of stops," the man informs you. "You won't arrive much before the regularly scheduled flight. And you won't be all that comfortable. But at least you'll make it tonight. Shall I enter your name on the passenger list?"

If you decide to take the mail plane, turn to page 15.

If you decide to take your chances and fly standby, turn to page 92.

"What does Gilroy have to do with uranium?" you ask.

"Before this amulet business, I had projected the location of the lost civilization of Satyrion in several scientific papers," your uncle explains.

"And this location," Major Winks adds, "is almost exactly aligned with new uranium deposits spotted by a high-powered American satellite called Infiltrator IV. We feel that the Brotherhood of Allah somehow found out about the satellite readouts and came here intending to overtake Gilroy's expedition and use it as a front."

"Incidentally," your uncle adds, "Bininuwuy, my tracker-friend, found the amulet slightly south of my projected destination."

You pause, trying to absorb all this information.

"So what's the plan?" you finally ask.

Turn to page 54.

"Thank you for coming," the stranger says, shaking your hand vigorously. As he speaks, Anna turns on a portable radio full blast. "Security precaution," the man assures you in a low voice. "We believe that this room is bugged."

"Where's my uncle? I want to know what's going on!" you demand.

"For a variety of complex reasons, your uncle has become the target of an international terrorist organization," the man replies patiently. "He is temporarily in hiding, under the protection of the Australian Intelligence Service. Anna and I work for the agency. My name is Jim Dodds. We have instructions to take you to see your uncle right now, if you are willing. However, we have also been instructed to inform you that if you decide to proceed, you may be facing real danger. Your very life could be at stake. It's my opinion that someone your age should not be exposed to such risks. But your uncle seems to think you can handle anything. It's up to you."

"Of course I'll come," you answer without a pause.

Jim and Anna nod in assent. Leaving the radio on, they take you down the fire escape and into the back of a furniture van waiting in an alley behind the hotel.

Turn to page 43.

The next morning, Major Winks fills you in on details.

"We will leave from here in four all-terrain vehicles at noon. It would be simpler to fly, of course, as your uncle did, but we want to give the Brotherhood of Allah a good chance to follow us.

"There will be eight of us altogether. I have arranged for a detailed story about the expedition, complete with maps, to be released to the press shortly after we depart. This will give us plenty of lead time. It will also give the enemy our exact location. We'll head into the Gibson for several hundred miles, then camp overnight. The uranium belt they're after is about six hundred miles from here. That will be our final destination," he finishes. "Any questions?"

Turn to page 64.

By this time it's growing dark. Hans and the old woman, whose name you still don't know, decide to keep searching for camels in the morning.

"What do you need camels for, anyway?" you ask.

"Shut up," one of the thugs beside you croaks.

That night they tie you to a bed. Despite your sore head, you're so exhausted that you sleep soundly.

You're woken by a small, popping sound. As you come to, it grows louder.

Gunfire! Your message must have gotten through!

Suddenly the door to the room bursts open. The old lady runs in with the business end of her revolver pointed in your direction. "This is all your fault!" she exclaims. "Traitor!"

"Traitor?" you repeat as she pulls her trigger.

Turn to page 74.

54

"Our plan is to stage a fake expedition and lure the terrorists into the desert after it," Major Winks announces.

"I'm your uncle's decoy, the 'substitute' Gilroy Adams," Jim Dodds says. Well, you think, that explains his uncanny resemblance to your uncle, and your own mistake back at the hotel. "I'll be heading the false expedition."

"Meanwhile, I'll be taking off in secret tonight to begin my dig where Bininuwuy found the amulet," Gilroy adds.

"What about me?" you ask.

"That's a good question," Major Winks replies. "We didn't reach your uncle until after he had called you from his hotel. Quite rightly, he already suspected that something was amiss. We think that the Brotherhood of Allah had the phone bugged. If this is the case, then your participation in the decoy expedition would lend that much more credibility. If you do participate, you will be making an invaluable contribution not only to the safety of Australia but to the world," adds the major. "I must repeat, though, that there is grave risk involved. If you choose not to go, you may accompany your uncle's expedition. While pursuing his own archaeological objectives, his team will provide support and backup to ours. That too has its dangers. Who knows what the Brotherhood would do if they uncovered our deception?" Major Winks finishes.

Turn to page 59.

56

You floor the accelerator and leap forward. Shouting comes from the direction of the fire.

Pling! Pling! Two bullets hit the rear of your Jeep, but you keep moving. You race through the desert night. One Jeep starts up. Then another. But soon their engines sputter, choke, and stop. That sugar trick was a good idea. It looks as though you've made it.

You continue driving through the night. You can't believe how still everything is. The only sound you hear is the occasional drone of a helicopter. When dawn finally arrives, Alice Springs is less than an hour off. Only a little farther to go and you'll be safe! You even begin to enjoy the wind blowing through your hair and the colors of the early sun against the rock and sand. Playfully you gun the Jeep over a rise and lift it into the air.

Turn to page 7.

"Thank you for your offer, but I think I'd better talk to the police," you say to the old man.

"Do what you must," he replies, and turns away.

You don't have time to apologize further. As quickly as possible you make your way to the Alice Springs police station and begin telling your story to an officer on duty. He looks as if he doesn't believe you.

"Here, look. These papers prove it!" you cry. You thrust the papers that you took from the man on the train into his hands.

The policeman looks at the papers. Without a word, he disappears into a rear office. You're not sure, but you think you hear him making a phone call. When he returns, he asks, "Where did you get these?"

Turn to page 73.

You sit next to Gilroy on the couch and notice for the first time that there are several other people in the room.

With a deep breath, Major Winks begins. "Approximately two weeks ago, Australian Intelligence received a tip that four members of the Brotherhood of Allah, an international terrorist group based in Libya, were about to enter the country. When the tip turned out to be true, our only question was what could they want with us? Unlike Europe or the States, Australia has had very little trouble with these types. But—needless to say—we placed them under closest surveillance anyway." Major Winks pauses. "It shortly became apparent that they came here for one thing: uranium."

"Uranium?" you say.

"Uranium to make nuclear weapons," Anna interrupts. "Almost every government in the world today fears that one of these groups will unlock the secrets of atomic weaponry. With enough uranium, they could ransom their target nations, or even the world!"

"Of course, the markets in uranium are strictly controlled. Getting hold of enough for a bomb is no easy feat," Major Winks goes on. "The one alternative these groups have is to acquire it from an entirely new source. For instance, a mine where no controls have been instituted—best of all, one that hasn't even been officially discovered. This is where your uncle Gilroy comes in."

Turn to page 50.

You look into Gilroy's face, but you can't tell what he's thinking. Everyone else is waiting quietly for you to make up your mind.

If you decide to go on the decoy expedition, turn to page 46.

If you decide to leave on the real expedition tonight, turn to page 68.

What a stroke of luck! You walk over to a quiet-looking beast and begin patting its side. "Don't look up while I talk," you say softly to the ranch hand. "I'm in a lot of danger."

"Huh?" the boy replies.

"I've been kidnapped by these people." You pretend to check the camel's mouth. "I was on my way to meet my uncle at the Barker House Hotel. His name is Gilroy Adams. Please call the hotel as soon as we're gone and tell him I'm being held hostage at thirty-one Ned Kelly Drive. Tell him to be careful."

"Hey! What's taking you so long?" Hans yells angrily.

"I don't think that this camel is any good," you call back to him. "In fact, none of them looks very good. I think we should try someplace else." Turning back to the boy, you repeat quietly, "Thirty-one Ned Kelly Drive. Please."

You run out of the paddock. Hans is so angry he cuffs you on the ear. "Don't leave us like that again!" he spits out angrily.

Turn to page 53.

As reality sets in, you're filled with panic. This is no decoy trip. These people are the very terrorists you've been warned against! And their ultimate goal is to create an atomic bomb.

You roll over in your bag. A few moments later, Anna shakes you gently, but you mumble something about being too tired to eat. You have some serious thinking to do.

Slowly you come to realize that you have two options—and neither one is safe. You can try to escape tonight in one of the Jeeps while the others sleep, or you can play along and look for a way to sabotage their plans, even if it means losing your own life.

Hours pass, and the camp grows quiet. It's time to make up your mind.

If you decide to attempt an escape by Jeep, turn to page 71.

If you decide to stay, hoping that some opportunity for overtaking this group will arise, turn to page 87.

"Look! There's my uncle!" you shout, pointing up the street.

Your four captors, falling for the oldest trick in the book, look in the opposite direction. In that split second, tearing across the road, you yell, "Help! I've been kidnapped! You have to save me!"

You are halfway to freedom when the icy hand of doom clamps onto your shoulder. It's the old lady! "She must lift weights," you think; her grip is so solid.

"My grandchild is a little unruly," she says sweetly to the staring kids. "Afraid of the dentist," she adds with a warm smile.

"You're not my grandmother! I never saw you before in my life!" you shout.

The kids start to laugh. They don't believe you!

One of the thugs has come to aid the old woman. There's no chance of getting away now, no matter how fiercely you resist. Back inside the car, Hans turns to you and says, "How very unfortunate, my young friend, that you tried to resist. If only you had cooperated."

Turn to page 41.

"What do we do once we get there?" you want to know.

"Since Jim will be posing as Gilroy, he'll go about what will appear to be normal archaeological pursuits," Major Winks explains. "The rest of us will go into hiding. We expect the Brotherhood to arrive within a day. Jim will be wearing a concealed tape recorder, and he'll use it to try to get proof of their intentions. While they're confronting each other, we'll come out of hiding, surround the area, and take them captive."

"We hope," you think.

Major Winks excuses himself, promising to answer any more questions later. The rest of the morning passes quickly as you pack the Jeeps for your trip. Spirits are high when you pull out of the corral at midday.

You are assigned to the Jeep driven by Anna. Your cargo includes most of the food and some water drums. The drive is dusty, hot, and dull. You are grateful for the first night's camp and the arrival of dusk. The sight of your bedroll makes you yawn hugely.

"Why don't you lie down for a little while?" Anna suggests. "I'll wake you when dinner is ready."

"Thanks," you say, curling up near the fire. Even with all the noise of camp, you fall asleep quickly.

Turn to page 37.

"I had kind of a disturbing trip up here," you tell Anna. "I'm sorry, but I don't feel that I can trust anybody right now."

"Have it your way." Anna shrugs. Then she turns and disappears in the throng.

You lug your bags to the taxi stand. "Barker House Hotel," you tell the dispatcher.

"I'm going to the same place," says a voice behind you. You turn around to see an old lady wearing a floppy hat and sunglasses. Her face is as dried and wrinkled as an apricot. She's carrying a shopping bag and looks like a tourist. "Why don't we share?" she suggests amiably.

Go on to the next page.

"Sure." You smile, relaxing a bit. Maybe you just have a case of nerves after all.

You climb into the cab and it pulls away from the curb. As soon as you are out of sight of the train station, the friendly old woman opens one of her bags.

"Where's that chocolate bar?" she mutters to herself. "I want some chocolate!"

But instead of chocolate, she pulls out a re-volver. Before you have a chance to react, she gives you a big grin—and thunks you on the head with the gun. Knocked out cold, you slump to the floor.

Turn to page 29.

"If you all don't mind," you say, "I'd like to stay with my uncle."

"Very well," Major Winks responds. You notice that he seems relieved. "I understand your decision. We can find someone to go in your place. And as I said, you will still be providing your country with a service by attending the support team.

"You will leave tonight," he continues. "We will drop you and a team of four agents near the amulet site with supplies, a radio, and food. Ground transportation should reach you from the south within twenty-four hours."

Winks goes over last-minute details and some maps with your uncle. Bininuwuy has temporarily disappeared. In the distance a plane engine starts up.

"Time to go," the major finishes, standing up. You walk into the black, moonless night toward a small landing strip behind the barns.

"Where's Bininuwuy?" Gilroy asks when you don't spot his face among the people loading the plane.

"Here I am," he says, emerging from the shadows.

The three of you climb in after the four other agents who will accompany you. "Have a good trip!" Winks yells.

Turn to page 84.

Very carefully you shuffle the papers together and replace them in the briefcase. It shuts with a small click, and you stand to leave.

"Where do you think you're going?" snaps a nasty voice.

You whirl around. The man has woken up!

"I've had it with you!" he yells, grabbing a fountain pen from his pocket and pressing a small button. It flashes through your mind that the pen is actually a gun, but just then a tall, thick-necked man appears in the doorway. So the pen must be a paging mechanism.

"Yes, boss?" says the man.

"Get rid of this kid. Quietly!"

"Wait a—" you begin to shout. But the goon clamps a rough hand over your mouth and drags you out of the compartment. His muscles are like steel. Kicking and struggling, you try to wriggle free as he carries you to the end of the car, but it's useless.

"Have a nice day," he says as he opens the door of the speeding train and throws you out into the starry Australian night.

The End

70

Hours later you wake up. Although you're aching all over, you seem to be unhurt. Groaning, you sit up and look around.

You've crashed somewhere in the desert. The rain and thunder have stopped, but the wind is still blowing fiercely.

Your eyes travel slowly over the interior of the plane. Gerry was thrown to the rear of the cabin. You can tell by the sickening angle of his neck that it's been broken. He's dead.

At first you don't see Ed. Then you realize that he is lying crumpled under some equipment that fell out of an overhead storage compartment. As you watch, he rolls over. "My leg," he moans. You give it a quick look. It's obviously been smashed—you can't tell how badly—and Ed seems to be in shock. But otherwise he looks uninjured.

You search the cabin for some water and find a couple of gallon jugs under a seat next to Gerry's body. As far as you can tell, there's no food.

"Here, drink this," you say, lifting Ed's head.

He slurps the water weakly. "Not too much. We don't know how long a rescue might take," he says, sinking back and closing his eyes.

Turn to page 24.

Rising on one elbow, you pretend to look into the fire, but in reality, you take stock of the situation. Good. Everyone is accounted for. And asleep.

You rise slowly from your bedroll. With enormous relief, you discover that the keys are in the ignition of Anna's Jeep. There's just one small thing to do before you leave. You find some sugar among the unpacked food. As quietly as possible you pour some into the gas tanks of the three remaining Jeeps. Even if they do wake up and start to come after you, they won't get far.

Taking a deep breath, and silently thanking your grandfather for teaching you to drive at such a young age, you turn the key.

The engine sounds like an explosion against the still night air. You're sure the others have awakened, but you don't dare turn around to look.

Turn to page 56.

"I stole them from this man on—" you start to say, but the officer interrupts.

"I'm afraid you're under arrest for possessing stolen information of crucial importance to national security."

"Under arrest?" you cry. "But they're after my uncle. It says so right here. They want to kill him! They want to neutralize him!"

"Explain that to the judge in the morning," answers the officer as he snaps handcuffs on your wrists.

The End

At that same moment, a police officer leaps through the doorway and hurls himself at the old woman. Her bullet is knocked off course. It only grazes your side. Gilroy, who runs in right after the policeman, calls for a medic. Then he quickly unties your hands and feet.

"I guess I messed things up, huh?" you say sadly, rubbing your sore wrists.

But your uncle tells you that the expedition has been called off altogether.

"Bininuwuy, the man who found the amulet, says that the tribal elders have warned against going. They say that the world must wait a few more months for the secrets of Satyrion," Gilroy says. He seems amazingly composed about it all.

"But what happens if someone else finds it first?" you ask. "Your life's work—your whole reputation—could be stolen by a rival!"

"Oh, don't worry. The tribal elders have already taken care of that. They've laid a protective spell. Until they lift it, no one will find Satyrion," Gilroy announces matter-of-factly.

"I suppose it's back to boring old Melbourne to finish my summer vacation," you say with a sigh.

"Not necessarily," Gilroy says, lighting his pipe. "There are recent reports of old cave dwellings inside volcanoes in the Atherton Highlands. I thought I'd take a look. Want to come?"

The End

Neutralized? Isn't that another word for killed? you wonder. Your uncle Gilroy *is* in trouble. Someone wants him dead! And that someone is on this train.

Leaving everything behind except your wallet and the stolen papers, you take off in the direction away from the car where the man with the briefcase is sleeping. You don't know what you're going to do until you come to a freight car.

That's it! You'll hide in there!

You wedge yourself between a shipment of carpets and one of lawnmowers. It's pretty uncomfortable, and you only sleep fitfully for the rest of the night. At least no one bothers you.

When the train stops in Alice Springs, the passengers get off on one side. You wait till they've left, then get off on the other side and sneak across the train yard. You're exhausted. You wish you could take a cab, but you decide it would be too risky. After a hot, dusty, and frightening walk through Alice Springs, you finally reach the lobby of the Barker House Hotel.

"Excuse me," you say to the receptionist. "Can you please give me the room number of Gilroy Adams?"

She eyes your dusty face and clothes with a bit of suspicion, but she checks her computer. "He's in room ninety-eight. But his key is here, which must mean he's out. Would you like to leave a message for him?"

"No, I'll wait," you say.

Turn to page 39.

"*Aaaaaaaaaaugh!*" you yell at the top of your lungs, while fleeing from the room.

"Wait! Please!" Anna yells, running after you.

You're barely looking where you're going. You tear through the hall, the thud of Anna's feet just a few steps behind.

You head for the lobby at top speed. But you forget about the stairs—and suddenly you're soaring through the air. Several patrons stare up from below, horrified, as you fly toward them.

You land on the marble floor with a sickening crunch.

Turn to page 22.

The old man points west, in the direction of the desert. "They went to track down more amulets," he announces.

"But—but that's impossible!" You just *know* Gilroy wouldn't leave without you. Maybe he's in some kind of trouble!

"Was there anything suspicious about the way they left?" you inquire.

"No. They were in a hurry. But that uncle of yours is always in a hurry." The man chuckles fondly. Then, turning serious, he adds, "If you're worried, we can go after them. I know where they were headed. We can leave right now."

You consider the man's offer. You feel that you've got to warn your uncle as soon as possible. But who can tell how long a trip into the desert will take? How safe would it be? And does this man know what he's talking about? Maybe you should try getting help from the police.

If you decide to accept the old man's offer to take you to your uncle, turn to page 100.

If you decide that it's time to involve the police, turn to page 57.

"So why are you here?" you ask.

"To try to prevent it from happening again. Humans are not as advanced in this evolutionary cycle as they were in our own. Ten years ago we decided to come down and see what we could do to help the planet, to awaken people to the danger before them," she answers. "We have done all we can. We have planted the seeds. The rest is up to you."

While Fifi has been talking, a gangplank was lowered from the glowing craft in front of you. The people in the crowd are starting to board the spaceship. Fifi and her friend edge toward it.

"But what can I do?" you cry. "I don't want Earth to die!"

"You must convince people to draw on the energy within. This life of power over things, the kind of power that nuclear energy represents, is far from the true nature of mankind. It is this that people must learn."

When Fifi finishes speaking, she turns and follows her friend into the light at the top of the gangplank.

Turn to page 88.

You scoop up as many papers as you can without touching the man's foot. Heart pounding, you dash through three cars to your compartment, where you lock the door behind you. Turning on a small flashlight, you start to read.

It all makes more sense this time. The classified report describes the location of a rich bed of uranium ore in the Gibson Desert. Then it explains that there's a connection between this recent discovery and the earlier claims of a young archaeologist—Gilroy T. Adams—who believes that the lost city of Satyrion once existed in the same area.

You're not sure what all this means, but the significance of a handwritten note in the margin is very clear.

"Adams may be a help. If not, he must be neutralized."

Turn to page 75.

It's Uncle Gilroy! And Bininuwuy! They must have figured out what Anna and the others were up to at about the same time you did. Thank heavens for your smart uncle—and for the thirty armed troops from Australian Special Forces that are backing him up.

"Hands up and march forward one at a time," barks the commanding officer.

Sheepishly the seven terrorists comply. The next hour is a blur of military interviews as you tell your story again and again. Helicopters arrive to transfer the prisoners to a military confinement center, where they'll await trial.

Turn to page 86.

82

The next day, after reaching the cacti, you and Bininuwuy change Jeeps. Then you pause for a minute to look at the cacti. They *are* strangely shaped—twisted into configurations that seem almost human. You can't help wondering if there's something supernatural about them.

"Good luck!" Gilroy calls as you drive off with Fifi.

The location 2.7 miles north-northeast lies on the far side of an outcropping of rock. You have to drive over rough terrain to reach it, and it takes longer than you planned to get there.

The desert sun drops fast. You don't have time to do much before dark except set up camp and build a fire. Fifi works busily. For some reason she keeps smiling mysteriously to herself. The last thing she says to you before going to sleep is, "You know the way back, don't you?"

This strikes you as an odd question—but, yes, you assure her, you know the way back.

Turn to page 90.

You've heard that some aborigines have extraordinary psychic powers. Mandarg may be right. But what's Gilroy up to? And why didn't he wait for you at the hotel? You lie in the dark thinking about all this for a few minutes, but you fall sound asleep without coming to any conclusions.

At dawn an urgent hand on your shoulder shakes you awake.

"We've got to go!" Mandarg says. "Bad things have happened to our friends. They have been betrayed by some people they trusted. The only people who can help them now are the police."

His face is twisted with sorrow and worry. You have no doubt that he's right—however it is that he knows these things.

You head back to Alice Springs immediately. The cool morning air helps you move quickly, and you reach the town not much after eight.

Even though it's early, police headquarters is in an uproar.

"Whaddya want?" the receiving officer asks you impatiently, ignoring Mandarg entirely. "And this better be good. We're awfully busy today."

"This is very important," Mandarg says imperiously, looking down his nose at the seated policeman. "We are looking for a missing man. He and a tracker from my tribe have been kidnapped by the Brotherhood of Allah."

This is news to you. But it has an amazing effect on the police officers. Within seconds, the entire room is silent. Everyone is staring at Mandarg.

Turn to page 89.

The flight to the amulet site takes an hour. The roar of the engine makes conversation or further questions useless. When you land, everyone works quickly to unload the drums of water and boxes of equipment and food. You are busy unpacking a tent when you hear a shout. "Okay, we're taking off."

You look up. Something is wrong! Everyone is back on the plane except for you, Gilroy, and Bininuwuy.

"Wait!" you scream, running after the plane. But the four agents just laugh and wave.

Turn to page 31.

"Where's my uncle?" you ask finally, not seeing him around. You scan the horizon.

Then you hear a whoop of triumph. Gilroy emerges excitedly from the opening that was spotted earlier.

"This isn't any mine! It's an entrance to the lost city of Satyrion! The discovery of the century!" he yells.

The End

"There's bound to be some chance over the next few days to stop these people," you think. Or at least to get a message out to the Australian government. For the first time you wonder about Gilroy and Bininuwuy. But it's useless to waste energy worrying about people you can do nothing to help. You have enough troubles of your own.

The next morning everyone acts normally. You've fooled them this far, at least. They probably don't even know you woke up yesterday. It takes all of your willpower to appear nonchalant as Major Winks gives you another briefing on the Brotherhood of Allah. At least you manage to learn the location of the shortwave radio. And by the way two of Winks's men are guarding one of the Jeeps, you strongly suspect that it contains explosives and weapons.

That day, you fold camp quickly and take off. Progress is slower as the track disappears and you travel over open terrain. Anna has to consult her topographical map frequently. Finally Major Winks signals for everyone to halt.

"According to my calculations, this is it," he says, indicating the area ahead with a sweep of his arm.

"Hey! Look!" someone yells from another Jeep. "That opening looks like the entrance to an old mine! Or a cave!"

Turn to page 97.

You watch in wonder as the large ball lifts into the air, hovers briefly, and zooms skyward. In a short while it is lost among the stars.

The next day you bring Gilroy to what remains of Satyrion. News of the reactor quickly makes headlines around the world.

You spend the rest of your life devoted to eradicating nuclear energy and weaponry of all kinds. If you are still alive to read this tale, you know your efforts have not been wasted.

Yet.

The End

"The Brotherhood of Allah? Can you lead us to their hideout?" the commanding officer steps forward to ask your friend.

"No, but I can lead you to Gilroy and Bininuwuy, and they know where it is," Mandarg says.

"Let's go," the man in charge says brusquely. He introduces himself hastily as you run to some helicopters behind the police station. He is Major Frank Symington, head of Australian Special Forces, Northwest Territory.

"Glad to meet you, Frank," Mandarg replies, giving you a mischievous smile.

You and Mandarg are hurried into separate helicopters, so you miss most of what Mandarg tells Major Symington. But an hour into the desert you spot a speck on the horizon and see Mandarg pointing. As you approach, you make out the shapes of a small camp and two people. One of them is your uncle Gilroy!

Turn to page 4.

You fall asleep not long after your head hits the pillow, but you are soon awakened. A strong wind is blowing sand in your face.

"Fifi, should we find better shelter?" you ask the huddled shape of the sleeping bag by the dying fire. "Fifi?" you repeat, getting up and shaking her.

But her sleeping bag is empty!

Turn to page 109.

Luck is with you. Four hours after you decide to fly standby, one of the passengers on the flight has to cancel, giving you a place just before the plane takes off. You're seated next to a friendly young man. Soon the two of you are talking about sailboats, school, and your favorite movies.

"Where are you headed?" you finally ask.

He pauses and gives you a funny, fleeting look. "I'm going home," he says. "What takes you to Alice?"

Gilroy didn't say anything about keeping quiet. After all, his expedition isn't exactly a secret. So you reply, "I'm going to meet my uncle—Gilroy Adams."

"The archaeologist?" the young man says in surprise.

"Yes. Do you know him?"

"We've never met, but I find his work very interesting," your seatmate replies. "His research into Satyrion is really brilliant. I don't care what anyone says."

You glow with pride at this compliment. "Gee," you say, "maybe Gilroy has room for another person. Would you like to come on the dig?"

The young man smiles, almost sadly, and says, "That's very kind. But I'm afraid I have previous obligations. Maybe another time."

Go on to the next page.

With that he opens a book and begins to read. The pilot announces your descent into Alice Springs. After landing, the young man shakes your hand warmly and disappears down the aisle.

Five minutes later, you're scanning the milling crowd for Gilroy when the man from your flight comes running over to you.

"Your uncle," he begins breathlessly, "your uncle will be looking in the wrong place. When you get into the desert, near the cacti, continue for another two-point-seven miles north-northeast. Good luck!" he adds. Then he rushes away.

You run after him as he skids around a corner, but he's gone. The hallway is empty!

Turn to page 20.

You spend the rest of the day on your hands and knees, while digging frantically. Ideas of magnificent wealth spur you on. By nightfall the vein of gold stretches for ninety feet. Who knows how far it goes? Who cares? By now you are the richest person in Australia, maybe in the world!

There's just one small problem. While you were busy digging, the remainder of your water evaporated in the heat. Over the next twenty-four hours, you die the slow, painful death of dehydration.

By the time you are gone, the wind has blown the sand over the gold vein again. No one would even know it was there.

The End

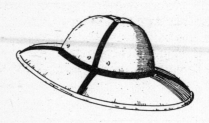

Just before you're about to ask if things will be okay, Gerry pulls out a paper bag and gets sick into it.

"Ed, I think it's something I ate. Food poisoning, maybe. I've never been airsick," Gerry says hoarsely before getting sick again.

"We both ate it, whatever it was," Ed replies. His skin is as pale as a sheet, and beads of sweat cover his brow.

Gerry doubles over with cramps.

Ed turns to you. "I'm afraid we're in trouble," he gasps. "Do you know anything about planes?"

At that moment you hit an air pocket, and the plane drops fifty feet.

"I only know a little. Tell me what to do!" you cry, as the plane dizzily swoops back up.

"Stay on one hundred eighty degrees—that dial there," Ed replies, indicating the controls. "Try to maintain altitude and make contact with Alice air traffic. They'll have to bring you in."

Ed says this last in a hoarse whisper. He looks as if he's beginning to lose consciousness.

"Alice Airport, please come in. Alice Airport, this is a mayday," you yell into the headset you've grabbed from Gerry.

BOOM!

Turn to page 32.

"What was the trouble, Gilroy?" you ask your uncle. "Does it have something to do with leaving so soon?"

"Exactly," Gilroy replies. "Things were just getting too weird for me. The press climbing in my window. Some crazy European arms dealers who wanted to purchase the formula for the polymer in the amulet to make plastic guns. Three mysterious people down at the aboriginal settlement looking for Bininuwuy. No camels to be had anywhere, when there are usually dozens available for an expedition. Finally, my room was searched this morning while I was out making calls. I'm pretty sure that my maps were photographed. We have to get out there to stake a claim as soon as possible."

"Who do you think it is?" you ask.

"I don't have any idea, but I could swear it's more than one group," your uncle replies. "Here we are," he adds, slamming on the brakes.

He pulls up alongside another Jeep where a man and woman sit waiting. "I'd like you to meet Ophelia and Bininuwuy," says your uncle.

Turn to page 21.

Everyone scrambles out of the Jeeps to look. All seven hover around a rock-strewn opening in the earth. They're talking and pointing excitedly. Now is your chance!

You sprint to the Jeep that was so carefully guarded. Sure enough, underneath a tarp, you find a crate full of machine guns. Grabbing one, you sneak up slowly on the crowd at the cave.

"Stay right where you are!" you yell fiercely. "Everyone raise your hands!"

Go on to the next page.

"What's going on?
Have you gone mad?" Major Winks
cries, turning around. "Put down the gun.
I'm afraid the heat has gotten to you."

He walks toward you. Aiming at a spot just in
front of his feet, you fire. Winks gets your point
quickly.

"You're wrong, mister. The heat has gotten to
you," you reply. "It got to you a long time ago
when you thought you could further your political
interests by killing innocent people. I want to an-
nounce to everyone in this so-called Brotherhood

that your terrorist days are over. You are under Australian citizen's arrest."

Major Winks lets out a huge belly laugh. "How do you propose to get all seven of us back to civilization?"

"With my help," says a familiar voice from behind you.

Turn to page 81.

100

You and the old man are quick to begin your journey into the desert. Along the way, the man tells you that his name is Mandarg. "I am the tribal elder of the Alice Springs settlement," he says. Other than that, he doesn't talk much, conserving his energy for the hot trek.

The two of you make good progress. At dusk you break for the day. Mandarg goes in search of some food while you start a fire. Later that evening, after a dinner of roasted lizard and several billies of tea, the two of you lie on your backs looking up at the stars. In a few minutes a small transport plane drones by.

Turn to page 104.

By nightfall you're glad of your decision. A sandstorm with gale-force winds whips up, and you have to use the plane for shelter. You huddle inside, trying to make Ed as comfortable as possible. He's a lot worse off than you first thought, and he keeps fading in and out of consciousness. You begin to fear some kind of internal bleeding.

Once, he wakes up slightly. "Please tell my parents I love them," he whispers.

"Come on, Ed," you say, "don't be morbid! You can tell them yourself as soon as you're well." But as his head drops back in your lap, you're not so sure.

Sometime during the night, you finally doze off. Early the next day you are awakened by the sound of a plane buzzing low overhead. A rescue!

Turn to page 111.

But you are not destined to find out.

Fifi fails to show up by dusk the next day. When you and Gilroy go in search of her, you find her Jeep abandoned exactly 2.7 miles north-north-east of the main camp. A cryptic note has been written in the dust on her dashboard: YOU ARE ALMOST THERE. KEEP ON LOOKING. GOOD LUCK.

Fifi's disappearance adds to the myth that continues to grow around Satyrion during your own long, distinguished career as you and Gilroy continue to search for the lost civilization.

The End

"It's my belief that Satyrion was an ancient civilization that existed when this continent was still part of the land mass that included Asia," Gilroy begins. "It was—with a few notable exceptions— very highly advanced. Several different sets of aboriginal cave paintings have been found, and clues from them indicate that the capital of Satyrion was located somewhere in the middle of what is now the Gibson Desert. In fact, I think the Gibson was created when Satyrion was destroyed in an incredibly powerful explosion."

This notion makes Gilroy pause to think. He knits his brows, shifts gears with a jerk, then mumbles something before continuing.

"My papers on Satyrion have become the butt of jokes in the archaeological community," Gilroy says, shrugging. "Let them laugh. I knew I would find it sooner or later. But Bininuwuy's find—that amulet—sped things up by ten years at least."

"How did he find it?" you want to know.

"Well," replies Gilroy, "Bininuwuy was on walkabout. Do you know what that is? The aboriginal custom?"

You shake your head.

"On walkabout," your uncle explains, "means taking a long trip on foot alone into the bush. Well, on his last walkabout Bininuwuy wandered into the Gibson."

"Into the desert? Alone?" you ask in amazement.

Turn to page 30.

"There they go now," says Mandarg dreamily, pointing above.

"There go who?" you ask.

"Bininuwuy and Gilroy. They're in that plane," Mandarg replies.

"In that plane? But I thought you said they left on foot. How can they be in that plane? And besides, how can you tell?" you cry.

"They did leave our settlement on foot. I don't know how they ended up in the plane. But they're there. My spirit eyes can see them." Mandarg seems as surprised about Gilroy as you do.

"Well, what else do you see? Are they okay?" you ask.

"They're all right for now. But my spirit will keep guard," Mandarg assures you.

Turn to page 83.

"So," says the woman from the cab as she marches into the room like a sergeant, "you've woken up."

She is followed by none other than the strange man with the briefcase—the man who ran into you on the train yesterday. Only today he is much more elegantly dressed, sporting riding jodphurs and a fancy pair of leather riding boots. A monocle glints at you from his left eye.

"We have a few questions for you," he announces with no further introduction. Again you notice his strange accent. "Why were you pestering me on the train yesterday?"

"Why was *I* pestering *you*?" you cry indignantly, wincing as you move your head for the first time. "Who ran into whom?"

"We ask the questions," snaps the old woman. "What was your reason for coming to Alice Springs?"

Now you have to think quickly.

"I come every summer," you say. "To visit friends. My best friend is here, in fact!"

"Do you know anything about camels?" the woman asks, peering into your good eye.

"Camels? Sure, I know about camels," you lie. "What else is there to do in Alice except ride camels?"

The man and woman laugh uproariously at this. "We can use this one to buy the camels for us, Hans," says the woman.

Turn to page 38.

"That's unbelievable!" your uncle exclaims after you have finished telling him about the man on the plane. "How could he know? Wait till I tell the others about this!"

That night, around the campfire, the four of you have a spirited discussion about the incident.

"I think he's trying to lead us off the track," Gilroy says excitedly. "We'll be on some wild-goose chase, and whoever planted this information will be digging in the spot *we* were headed to in the first place!"

"I don't know," Fifi replies thoughtfully. "There might be some truth to it. Why don't I go take a look? While I do that, you and Bininuwuy can begin the excavation near his original find at the cacti."

Gilroy nods slowly. "That's not a bad idea," he finally says.

"Do you want to come with me?" Fifi adds, turning toward you.

If you accept Fifi's offer, turn to page 82.

If you decide to stay with your uncle and Bininuwuy at the original dig site, turn to page 110.

You dash out into the blowing sand. "Fifi! Fifi! Where are you?" you yell. You run up a small rise to get a better view. There you stop, frozen in your tracks.

Below you, about a hundred yards in the distance, a huge glowing ball—six stories high—descending slowly to earth. Hundreds of people, all colors and shapes, ages and nationalities, stand clustered in front of it. In the rear of the crowd you spot a familiar figure.

"Fifi!" you call running down the hill. She turns toward you. A man she has been talking to turns as well. It's your seatmate from the plane!

"What's happening?" you cry, out of breath.

Just then a cheer breaks out in the crowd. The huge silver ball has landed.

Turn to page 112.

110

You break camp early the next morning and reach your intended destination by midday. No one seems to have been at the site before you. Gilroy is obviously relieved.

"This is where I leave you," Fifi says cheerfully. "I plan to dig through the day. I should be back here with news by tomorrow."

You feel a pang of regret as you watch the woman drive off alone. But it is quickly dispelled by digging in the hot desert sun under Gilroy's direction. You've never worked harder in your life.

By dusk, the three of you have uncovered several square feet around the cacti. Nothing has turned up.

"I wonder if Fifi has found anything," you say out loud before turning in for the night.

"We'll find out tomorrow," says Gilroy with a yawn.

Turn to page 102.

"Ed! We're saved!" you cry, nudging the pilot. But it's too late. His body has grown stiff with death.

You scramble out of the wreckage and wave frantically as the plane circles back. Tears are streaming down your face.

You are taken by the Australian Air Force rescue team to a military hospital, where you're treated for shock and exhaustion.

Your uncle visits you there. "I'm sorry," he says, "but I'm going to have to leave without you. I just can't wait any longer to start my expedition. I hope you understand." You do.

Turn to page 47.

"It's time for me to go, to return to where I came from," Fifi tells you gently.

"In this—this spaceship?" you ask. "Are you an alien?"

Fifi smiles a sad smile. Then you realize who she reminded you of earlier: the man standing next to her.

"I used to reside here on Earth. Before the accident," she says.

"We both did," the man from the plane adds. "As citizens of Satyrion in the height of its glory."

"What happened? What do you mean?" you cry.

"That was a wonderful time," Fifi begins. "Earth was even more magnificent than it is now. The governments were good, and fair. The abundance on the planet assured that no one went hungry. There was only one problem. Nuclear energy."

"It was messy and dangerous, but cheap," her friend tells you. "Many of us fought against its use, but to no avail. We could see the end coming. We were forced to move to a friendly planet not half as wonderful as this in order to survive."

"Not long after we left, the holocaust came. Life was extinguished on Earth," Fifi goes on. "The epicenter of the blast was here in the capital. The hull of the old reactor is right over there," she adds, pointing to a ruin nearby.

Turn to page 78.

"Bininuwuy, you old weasel!" Your uncle laughs, clapping his friend on the back. He replaces the batteries, and the radio whines to life. "S-O-S," your uncle says into the mouthpiece. "Can anyone read me? S-O-S."

A short while later, Gilroy has related the entire story to a cattle rancher located southwest of Alice Springs. The rancher promises to phone the police and the military immediately.

"Hooray!" you cry as your uncle signs off. "We're saved! The world is saved! Now there's nothing to do except wait for our rescue!"

"What do you mean, 'nothing'?" your uncle says, smiling and handing you a shovel. "Bininuwuy found the amulet right over there. We've got some digging to do!"

The End

ABOUT THE AUTHOR

Shannon Gilligan graduated from Williams College in 1981. While a student, she spent a year studying at Doshisha University in Kyoto, Japan. When she's not traveling to do research for her books, she lives in Vermont.

CHOOSE YOUR OWN ADVENTURE®

Special Offer
Buy a Bantam Book
for only 50¢.

Now you can order the exciting books you've been wanting to read straight from Bantam's latest catalog of hundreds of titles. *And* this special offer gives you the opportunity to purchase a Bantam book for only 50¢. Here's how:

By ordering any five books at the regular price per order, you can also choose any other single book listed (up to a $5.95 value) for only 50¢. Some restrictions do apply, so for further details send for Bantam's catalog of titles today.

Just send us your name and address and we'll send you Bantam Book's SHOP AT HOME CATALOG!